PRISON TALES
STORIES FROM THE INSIDE

K.C.

Bloomington, IN  Milton Keynes, UK
authorHOUSE®

AuthorHouse™
1663 Liberty Drive, Suite 200
Bloomington, IN 47403
www.authorhouse.com
Phone: 1-800-839-8640

AuthorHouse™ UK Ltd.
500 Avebury Boulevard
Central Milton Keynes, MK9 2BE
www.authorhouse.co.uk
Phone: 08001974150

This book is a work of fiction. People, places, events, and situations are the product of the author's imagination. Any resemblance to actual persons, living or dead, or historical events, is purely coincidental.

© 2007 K.C.. All rights reserved.

No part of this book may be reproduced, stored in a retrieval system, or transmitted by any means without the written permission of the author.

First published by AuthorHouse 5/27/2007

ISBN: 978-1-4259-6738-3 (sc)

Library of Congress Control Number: 2006909642

Printed in the United States of America
Bloomington, Indiana

This book is printed on acid-free paper.

DEDICATION

I'd like to dedicate this book to my father, who also had a passion for writing but never had a chance to show it to the world.
In loving memory of Kevin Dukes.

ACKNOWLEDGEMENTS

First and foremost I'd like to thank GOD for giving me the ability to be talented on paper. To my husband, you are my inspiration and my rock thanks for being patient. To my mother who also loves to write, thanks for passing that onto me. You believing in me made it possible for me to believe in myself. To my baby girls… you guys are my strength, the reason why I continue to push and strive to do my best especially at being your mom. To all my family and friends who helped me out along the way. I love you all. To Author house for helping make my dream come true.

CONTENTS

CONDEMNED	1
DEATH ROW	7
FIGHTING TO SURVIVE	15
CAUGHT UP	21
JUST HAVING FUN	43
TILL DEATH DO US PART	49
WORKING ADDICT	57
I`M INNOCENT	69
OUT OF THE PAN AND INTO THE FIRE	73
NOT AGAIN	81
STOLEN INNOCENSE	89
BOOTY BANDITS	125
WHAT I WOULDN`T DO	131
LIFE LESSONS	145
SEEK AND YOU SHALL FIND	167

CONDEMNED

It's cold dark and damp. I'm hungry and disoriented. Where am I? How long have I been here? I'm huddled in a corner, knees are to my chest, arms hugging my knees shivering, trying to figure out my whereabouts. Out of nowhere this blinding bright light comes on and it stings my eyes then someone shouts "NAME AND NUMBER!!" As it all comes flooding back to me again someone shouts "NAME AND NUMBER!!" Valerie Jones…3210501234 then the lights go out and I am left alone with my memories. Bits and pieces of my memory start to come back to me in frightening flashes.

OH MY GOD…I'M IN JAIL! I yell out to no one in particular. I fight to remember why? Where is my son? Who is watching over my precious boy? A voice in my head answers… GOD is watching him now.

I feel panic setting in.

What are you talking about?

I want to see my boy. What has happened to him?

Please tell me. The voice again speaks, "don't worry anymore he is safe in GODS arms. You made sure of that. What do you mean? how.. what.. I don't understand…please I want to see my boy! Let me hold him. The voice "YOU CAN'T, HE'S DEAD!" a SCREAM COMES FROM SOMEHWERE DEEP INSIDE OF ME NNOOOOO..THAT'S A LIE..

YOU'RE A LIAR!!! BEN!...Ben! Don't you hear your mama calling you? Ben come to me...I love you... where are you Ben? I hear my son's voice...mama? I look up and some where in the darkness I can see my son. Come here baby I say to my seven year old, let mama hold you. Slowly he comes closer to me and he keeps saying "why mama why...?" I can see him clearer now. He has been beaten, black and blue and covered in blood. What happened to you? Tell me who did this. Again, he says "why mama?" I'm fighting to understand... the voice, angry now says "look at him! Look what you've done!!"

In horror I answer, "I could never do anything like that to someone I love so dearly." "the YOU you used to be before you married crack and became his whore loved Ben but the crack whore you became didn't give a fuck about him!!" I felt fresh hot tears roll down my face as I remembered what happened. I became violently sick as the images of what I allowed to happen to my son flashed in my head. I pimped my son to whoever would pay me so I could get my drugs. I forced him to lay down with grown men to get what I needed. When he didn't do as the paying customers asked I beat him, sometimes until he bled. On occasion a customer would pay double to beat him. That was a good day. While he cried and rubbed his bruises I would get so high I couldn't remember my own name. The horrible images that flashed before my eyes started to slow down. No more I said to the voice. I can't take anymore, I don't want to remember.

"Oh, you can't take anymore…what about your precious son?" You didn't stop to think that maybe he couldn't take anymore. One last image flashed of my son lying dead in a crack house naked on a dirty mattress bruised and bloody with a needle sticking out of his arm. I heard him say once again before I blacked out only to wake up in my own hell and relive my past day after day…"Why Mama, why?"

DEATH ROW

I was given a death sentence before I was born. My mother was a black crack addicted whore. The only thing she ever gave me was AIDS then she died. Only God knows who my father was. In my world there was no such thing as love and patience. Nobody cared what happened to me, so why should I?

I bounced from foster home to foster home until I was ten. I never had foster parents that cared they just did it for the money. They took the money that they were given to care for me and used it for there own personal gain. At ten I started to speak out and ask for the basic things I needed to take care of myself and that's when I was shipped off to a group home. In the group home somebody finally taught me something.

The other boys would jump me every chance they got. They stole what few possessions I owned. They taunted me about my disease. So let me tell you what I've learned.

I learned to hate and not give a fuck about anyone or anything. By the time I was sixteen I was withdrawn, and full of rage. As the years past with no one to talk to I just got worse. A walking time bomb just waiting to explode. One day that's exactly what I did. In a couple of months I would be eighteen. The group home said I had to find a job and a place to live.

Everyday they gave me a metro card and a newspaper then sent me on my way. No training, no nothing. How was I suppose to know how to act on an interview? I've never been on one let alone had a job. I was determined to get out of this hell hole and learn how to stand on my own two feet and make something of myself.

In the beginning I was excited and I tried real hard. Everyday I went out and everyday I was told I had no skills, not enough education or I was unqualified. What little hope I had was stomped out of me with each interview.

One week before my eighteenth birthday after another failed

interview I was sitting on the steps of a run down abandoned brownstone in Harlem.

I was mad at the world trying to figure out what to do. NO JOB, NO MONEY, NO HOME AND NO FAMILY, I had nothing. The group home was kicking me out in a matter of days. How was I going to survive?

As I was sitting there wishing I could just die this girl walked by and she looked at me with such disgust while mumbling something under her breath as she rolled her eyes and turned her nose up at me. She thought she was better than me. My self pity turned to hatred and rage.

My whole shitty life flashed before me and I snapped. In that girl

I saw my crack whore mother who abandoned me, the boys who beat me down every chance they got and I hated HER for it. I needed to blame someone. Someone needed to pay for the fucked up life I was living in and she was there.

I snatched her up dragged her into the building by her hair and neck. She was kicking and screaming. I beat her like she stole from me. I kicked and punched her in the stomach and back until she stopped fighting. She just laid there with this look on her face. She was taunting me so I ripped the clothes off her body and tied her hands with her shirt to a radiator. When I got down to her bra and panties and she realized what I was about to do she started to panic. Pleading and begging for me to stop. All I wanted her to do was shut the fuck up!! But she wouldn't so I pulled down my pants and shoved my dick in her mouth over an over until I came. She stopped trying to talk. After that I tore off her bra and panties. As she slipped in and out of consciousness I pushed her legs apart and tore into her with a vengeance. I heard her rip as I forced my way in. I hated her for every wrong turn my life took. She cried out in pain every time I slammed into her. The more she cried the harder I pounded. I shoved and pounded myself in and out of her over and over until I exploded. I was drained of all energy, hate and rage. Exhausted, drenched in blood and sweat, I blacked out.

I woke up shackled to a hospital bed in the county jail waiting to be sentenced.

The judge saw fit to sentence me to death. I had given the girl a death sentence of her own.

AIDS.

FIGHTING TO SURVIVE

When you Live on the streets you never know when your gonna eat. Sometimes I got lucky and the shelter had room. That's considered a real treat. I got to shit, shower and shave in a warm dry place. If I got there early enough I got a hot meal and a place to rest my head.

The winter time is the worst. The shelters are over crowded with women, their children and the elderly. I almost never get in. Being a young single man doesn't help. People are dying on the streets every night freezing to death.

Three hots and a cot sound good to me especially after trying to survive outside in the cold. I don't understand what all the complaining and whining is about when people get locked up.

My name is John and I'm homeless. Every year at the end of Fall I get locked up on purpose just to stay alive. A petty crime like a robbery gives me just enough time to get out in the Spring.

In my eyes prison is my savior. It's not the Hilton but I get a hot shower, clean clothes and free medical and dental. In the street you don't get any of that not even if you have a job. Last year when I went in I found out that I had pneumonia. They fixed me with some simple medications and when I was better they gave me a needle to prevent me from getting it again for five years. Where else can you go to get free food, housing, clothing, medications and an education if you want it? You can even get a job. It doesn't pay much but it's enough to put money on my books. I can get anything I want from commissary. On the streets I can't do for myself anymore. That makes me feel less than a man. In jail if you do what you're supposed to do, keep your eyes open and your mouth shut life can be sweet. I couldn't ask for more. Instead of letting the system get to me and break me down I make the system work for me.

If you would've asked me five years ago how I felt about the prison system my answer would have been totally different. Five years ago my life took a turn for the worse. Nine eleven...I lost my wife in one of the buildings. Her remains where never found. My job was lost when the second building went down and everyday I wish I didn't have that day off. We never had any children and before nine eleven it was something that caused tension between us and now I think it was a blessing in disguise. What little money I had went quick and the bills kept coming. When the money was gone I tried to get help but they caught some people scamming right before I applied and things were shut down. I was denied everything I applied for...and they call this the land of the free??? In order to get aid in this country you have to be a foreigner or be stripped of everything. You have to have absolutely nothing before they even consider giving you any kind of help.

One day I went out for a job interview and came home yet again without a job. Just when I thought it couldn't get any worse I found myself without a home. There was a large pad lock on the door, my home and my possessions all gone.

My life changed forever. I did things I never thought I would do to survive.

CAUGHT UP

The first thing I need and want to do is apologize to my Mama. I know that Big Mama did the best she could by me and my four other siblings. My birth mother started having us when she was fifteen years old. My being the first-born I am the oldest and the only girl. She kept having babies every two years. My grandmother tried to keep us all together including my mother but that was impossible. My mother left when my youngest brother was just two years old.

K.C.

Never said a word to us just got up one morning and left.

I helped big mama as much as I could. She worked three jobs in order to put food on the table, clothes on our backs and a roof over our heads. While she did that I held it down at home. I made sure all homework was done, the house was clean and I kept my brothers in line. We made a good team, our system worked for us but I guess it was just too much for Big Mama. Now that I think about it she was up in age and she was always tired. One night she came home from work sat down at the kitchen table fell asleep and never woke up. The doctor said she had a massive heart attack.

Family was the most important thing to Big Mama so I tried to honor that after she was gone. I dropped out of school and got two jobs in order to take over Big Mama's role. My sixteen year old brother stepped up and took my place at home. I made him promise to stay in school. He was an A student so that wasn't a problem. For the first year we worked together like a well-oiled machine. Don't get me wrong we were tired but the bills were paid. Everybody's belly stayed full and our clothes were neat and clean. Somewhere along the line we dropped the ball. My brother started smelling himself. "I'm a man now and I need time for myself" is what he said. He took the time and the little ones felt the neglect.

I got a call one night from the local precinct telling me that my brother was locked up for assault and battery. That meant the kids were home alone doing God knows what. I asked my boss for an emergency leave. He said, "If you walk out on me tonight don't come back." Needless to say I lost my job. I went to see my brother because I couldn't believe he would ever hurt anybody. The charge was not of his character. He confessed to me, said he was defending himself. Some guy came at him over some girl. I should have known he'd gotten his first piece of pussy when he started acting out. I just wish it were from somebody who was worthy of him. The bitch he chose definitely wasn't. She was playing him against some drug dealer and got busted. When the other guy saw them together he got all up in miss girls face and my brother defended her and it landed him in jail. Our lives spiraled downward from that point on. I tried to work, keep house and take care of the kids but I couldn't do it all. I got fired from my other job for sleeping. I went to the City to try and get help with food and money. They turned me down. Told me I didn't have legal custody of the kids so they were not my responsibility. I couldn't believe what I was hearing. The lady also told me that I was young and there was no reason I couldn't get a job. She obviously didn't have any kids. I left there in tears. I wondered the streets for hours crying and trying to think of a way to keep my family together. Tired and hungry I ended up in some kind of bar that served food. Sitting down at the bar I ordered an appetizer and a double rum and coke. After I finished my order and my drink I felt ten times better. I went to pay my bill and realized that I had lost the rest of my money. Sitting there penniless I didn't know what to do. The man on the other side of the bar must have been watching me the whole time because when I started checking and rechecking my pockets he came over and propositioned me. He offered to pay my bill if I repaid it by working in his club. I said yes and thanked him without getting any details. He paid my bill and off we went to his club. He told me he wanted me to start tonight. I had no idea what I had signed myself up for. We arrived at his club in minutes. When we entered I couldn't believe my eyes. There was half naked woman everywhere, some walking around serving drinks others dancing on stage. At a quick glance around I saw two men being led to the back to private rooms to do GOD knows what. Turning back to the man who owned this place with fear in my eyes I said, "I can wash dishes, bartend, even cook but I-I-I can't do anything else, I'm not qualified." My dear you are

K.C.

mistaken, you definitely have all the right qualifications to work here. With that smooth caramel skin those light brown eyes that itty-bitty waist and that beautiful long jet-black shiny hair that could touch that big ass of yours if you hold your head back at the right angle. I was speechless. He looked at me with lust in his eyes licked his lips and said with a smile, "besides, you owe me." Where else can you get a job that pays a hundred dollars a night plus tips tax free? That'll work I thought. I could catch up on the bills, buy new clothes for the boys, go food shopping and even get a sitter so that I could work without worrying. This may not be so bad after all. Okay, what do I have to do and when do I get paid? Since you're new I'll start you off slow. Let's go into my office to discuss the details. As we walked to his office he ordered two double rum and cokes from a passing barmaid slapped her on her ass and sent her on her way.

Once inside he told me to take off my jacket and relax. First thing we have to do is give you a stage name. Let's see, hmmm he pondered for a moment....I got it. We'll call you "Cinnamon". At that moment the drinks arrived. The barmaid placed them on the table and left quietly closing the door behind her. Okay, get undressed. I clammed up again. I-I thought you said we'd take it slow. He sighed, slightly irritated and said I told you to relax.

Here, drink this. He handed me a double rum and coke and I downed it. Look, I can't put you out there without checking you out first. You don't expect to go out there dressed like that do you? Besides you have to pass inspection. You do want this job don't you? I didn't but I did need that money. As if he read my mind he said you'd get paid at the end of each night you work I looked at him and said you mean…Yes you'll get paid tonight if you pass inspection minus your dinner bill he said smiling. Now can we get down to business? I stood up with my back to him took a deep breath closing my eyes and did as I was told. As I started to undress music started to flow through the speakers. It helped me to relax. I heard him say feel the music let it take you. By then my two double rum and cokes started to kick in. Never opening my eyes, I started to sway to the music…undress to it. After I removed the last article of clothing I could feel him close to me. His breathe on the back of my neck. He reached around me and caressed my breast then he pinched my nipples just hard enough to make them stand at attention. I could hear someone breathing heavily as he kissed my neck and caressed my flat belly. As he reached the top of my pubic hair line I quivered. He whispered in my ear to open my eyes. I did as I was told. The lights had been dimmed and to my surprise the breathing I heard was my own. He told me I had passed the first part of my inspection and for the last part I would need to lie down so I did. I watched him watch me part my legs. He ran his fingers lightly up my things sending a bolt of electricity thru my entire body. The closer his hand got to my pussy the more nervous I became because I had never been touched there by anyone. I was still a virgin. Before I could protest he said that I had passed and that I could get up. I breathed a sigh of relief. He left me momentarily only to return with a skimpy outfit for me to work in. Tonight I'm going to start you out as a server. The patrons are allowed to touch you as long as they are not rough or disrespectful. I advise you to get dressed, finish your drink and relax. The more relaxed and friendly you are, the more tips you will make. You have beautiful teeth try smiling. Come out when you are ready and one of the girls will show you the ropes, with that he left closing the door behind him.

The first couple of weeks flew by so fast. I was in the swing of things. I made some friends and most of the customers were regulars so I got to know them too. I actually liked my new job and the money was good but greed got the best of me. I knew I could make more money and I was ready. I told my boss that I was ready for a promotion, a private dancer which is one step away from top pay. I was excited and nervous. Starting tonight I would get a new title, two hundred dollars a night plus tips. Just thinking about my salary put me on a natural high. Private dancers had to buy their own outfits. I could have purchased something from the house mom on the premises but I wanted something special. I didn't want to look like any of the other dancers so I dipped into my stash and went to the village. I spotted this hot pink little number that had my name written all over it. I went in and tried it on. It had a floor length cover up, spaghetti straps, heart shaped bodice that fit my breast like a glove. The gown fell to my ankles. The bottom part was all fringes from my butt to my feet. It came with hot pink and black garter belts and a matching thong. It was the most I've ever spent on one outfit for myself but I figured I was worth it. I purchased some make up, matching accessories and a fringed whip to complete the look. I was ready for tonight. Returning home I made two CD's with all my favorite music. Since each session only lasted about fifteen minutes I had more than enough.

I cooked for the boys and called the sitter. I changed the polish on my fingers and toes to match my outfit. Shaved in all the right places washed my hair and soaked in the tub to try to get rid of my jitters. I figured I'd wear my hair wet and wild a change from the straight look. I was still too nervous to sleep so when the sitter came I kissed the boys, threw my garment bag over my shoulder and caught a cab to the club. The first thing I did was order two double Rum and cokes to get rid of my bad nerves. The drinks definitely did the trick. By the time they made the announcement that I was available for private dances I was good and loose.

My first customer was one of my regular patrons, which made it so much easier on me. He placed a fifty on the table and sat back ready to enjoy his view. It was a definite plus that I was very attracted to this man. I have been for weeks. He brought out feelings in me I never knew existed.

Working in this club over the last couple of months I have seen a lot of freaky shit but still had yet to experience it. Today I was crossing over from watching and learning to doing.

I looked into his eyes and started my dance of seduction and when his time was almost up I had him mesmerized. I could tell he wanted me so I moved closer to him, teasing him with my body. Just as his time was up he slapped a hundred dollar bill on the table and asked what was allowed. Everything except penetration I whispered close to his ear. I am at your beck and call for the next twenty minutes. In that case slow down the music and come stand over me so I can smell you. I got right up in his face placing one foot on the side of his thigh and the other on the table, which positioned my pussy right at his nose. He pressed his nose in such a way that it parted my lips making my thong moist. He palmed my ass and took a long hard whiff. You smell good enough to eat he stated while pulling off my garment and tossing it to the floor. He slowly inserted one finger into me while he squeezed my ass and rubbed my clit with his nose back and forth. He found his rhythm, in and out one finger then two. It felt so good that it made me dizzy. I had to hold on to the straps that hung above his head to keep from falling. I always wondered what those straps were for. My body started to tense I felt like I was going to explode. No sooner said than done, my first orgasm. He pulled me down onto his lap and looked into my eyes. He was so hard I could feel him throbbing against me. His time was up and as I was about to move he placed two more bills on the table. Stay he said and I did. Where can I kiss you? Anywhere except my mouth. He began planting soft kisses all over my face then my neck. I can't believe I'm getting paid to feel this good. I wanted to kiss him but instead I just buried my head in his neck and started to kiss his neck and chest. I didn't know how much more I could take. I wanted him inside of me. As if he read my mind he whispered close to my ear, I've wanted you from the first day I saw you and I'm willing to pay. I can't….it's not about the money, I…he put five more bills on the table and started to grind his dick against my pussy with only my thong separating us. My body caught his rhythm and I started grinding on top of him against my better judgement. I heard my mouth saying no but my body had its own agenda. I was losing this battle. He laid me down on the table and pulled off my soaking wet thong. Baby I can't I protested while he put on a condom. Please he begged, just a little bit he breathed heavily. We shouldn't do this… we can't I panted. Without saying another word he pushed my legs up and dove head first between my legs.

While massaging my clit with his tongue he filled each opening with his fingers. I thought I was going to loose my mind. I was hooked on him. Again I climaxed. At that point I was pulling at him and begging him to put it in. Just as he was about to enter me he looked into my eyes and told me not to worry he would be gentle. How did he know? He eased in a little and it hurt. He rubbed my head and slowly worked his way in by going in and out a little deeper with each down stroke the pain stopped and it started to feel good. We were so into each other we didn't hear the commotion up front. Just as we came together cops in riot gear knocked down the door, weapons drawn they roughly pulled us apart and we were arrested. I was arrested for indecent exposure and prostitution and him for soliciting.

JUST HAVING FUN

Now that I look back on my life and the choices that I've made I guess you could call me naïve or just plain stupid. Ever since I took an interest in men from the age of thirteen, I've been a bum magnet. If there was a no good, good for nothing guy age fifteen and older who had a rep for using and abusing women within a block radius I wanted him and would do anything to get him.

When I started dating it was little things like giving my lunch money to the boy I liked just to get him to notice me. Once I lost my virginity at age fifteen it was a whole new ballgame. I wasn't even interested in having sex at that age but when I saw that I could get anything I wanted from a man like money, gifts and attention especially the attention I saw it as an even trade off. I didn't sleep around or anything like that. I had a boyfriend and from him I craved to feel wanted all the time.

At age sixteen I got myself a real bad boy. That was a big turn on for me. He was

out of school had his own ride and he was into guns. I'd never even seen a real gun until I met him.

One night we were out partying and a group of us were drinking and having fun riding around town. One of the other guys thought it would be fun to dare one of us to hold up a store so me, as stupid as they come volunteered. Me being young, dumb and drunk (what a bad combination) grabbed the gun from under the seat where my man kept his heat. I ran into the store waving the gun and yelling at the man behind the counter to give me all the money out of the register. He didn't respond he just stood there looking into the mirror that most stores have that lets you see the entire store and it's patron's in every isle. So I banged the gun on the counter to get his attention. " What are you deaf or just dumb?!! Give me the money or else!!" I yelled and screamed at him but he still didn't move, he just kept starring so I looked up to see what he was looking at. I froze in fear. There were two uniformed cops moving slowly towards me with there guns drawn. I silently panicked. What have I gotten myself into now! I looked at the front door and thought if I could just get out I'm sure I would get away because my friends never cut the car off. I could hear them just out side goofing around. I turned to run and only got a few steps before one of the cops let out a warning shot into the ceiling. After the gun sounded I heard the car screeching from the scene as it peeled out of the parking lot and sped away. At that moment I knew I would never see anyone in that car again. The cops ordered me to put my weapon on the ground **SLOWLY.** I did as I was told because although I lived a rebellious life I still wanted to live it. I was ordered to kick the gun towards them. After I did that they were on me with a quickness. They shoved me to the ground face down and handcuffed me behind my back. While we waited for a police car to arrive the female cop walked over to me and smacked me in the back of the head and said "what were you thinking?!!" I just sat there dumb founded because I wasn't thinking. At that moment I vowed to get my life in order.

TILL DEATH DO US PART

You reap what you sew. I think that statement was written just for me.

I was married to a beautiful woman once. When I met her she was vibrant and full of life. She had a smile that could melt anyone's heart. Arguing wasn't her style; she liked to keep the peace. I had the perfect wife; I just didn't realize it until it was too late. My house was always kept clean and she was a wonderful cook... not as good as my ma's but the next best thing. I could talk to her about anything. We used to talk for hours about any and every thing. A man couldn't ask for a better woman to have by his side.

On the other hand you had me... Mr. Greedy. Growing up I had a saying that I learned from my grandfather. "Young, dumb and full of cum" that was me. I stuck my dick in every chick that smiled my way. Cocky was my middle name so trying to hide my infidelities once I got married was something I never did. I just didn't give a damn. My wife begged and pleaded with me to change my way but it fell on deaf ears.

She put up with my behavior for so many years and each year my behavior got worse. Some nights I partied so hard I forgot I had a wife and didn't go home until the next afternoon. She would get so upset with me. I was "the man" all it took was some sweet talkin' and some extra good lovin'and all was right again. Somewhere along the line that stopped working and she gave up. I remember her telling me once that she didn't feel appreciated or loved and when I didn't respond she gave up on me. I on the other hand didn't get the hint for a couple of months because I was so wrapped up in other women.

One morning something snapped in me. I woke up in a strange place next to two women. I didn't even know their names. At that moment I got disgusted with myself and decided I didn't want to live like this anymore. I was going to turn over a new leaf. I jumped out of the bed and found the bathroom to shower. On the way home I decided to buy my wife some flowers seeing as I'd never done that in the seven years we'd been married. I suddenly felt bad about how I had treated her all those years. I really am a lucky man to have her because if the shoe was on the other foot I would have left her a long time ago. I swore to myself that I would make it up to her or die trying.

When I entered our home I couldn't believe my eyes. My wife was standing in the middle of the room soaking wet from head to toe. She was holding a piece of paper in her hand. At first glance I thought she had just gotten out of the shower but then an odor hit my nose ,then I noticed the empty gas can at her feet. I was horrified. I noticed she was crying as she held the piece of paper out to me. It was an HIV test and the results were positive. They were my test results. I had known for about six months now and I just didn't know how to tell her. I never used protection with anyone especially not her because she was my wife. I never thought protecting me meant protecting her as well, until now. My eyes filled with tears my heart with remorse. OH GOD what have I done! Baby...I'm sorry, don't do this... we can get thru this together please don't and before I could finish my sentence she went up in flames. Her screams were filled with pain. Her last words to me were "I HATE YOU

FOR WHAT YOU'VE DONE TO ME! You made my life a living hell when all I did was try to love you. I didn't deserve this death but you do" and with that she jumped out and grabbed me in a bear hug. As we burned together I fought to get her off of me. I wasn't ready to die.

My wife died in that fire. I may as well have joined her for the kind of life that I'm left with.

In case your wondering how I ended up in jail, my wife made a call to the police and told them that I intentionally gave her AIDS and that I threaten to set her on fire. They arrived with an ambulance just in time to save my life. I have third degree burns on eighty percent of my body. My hair that was once shiny and wavy only grows out of a small patch on the side of my head. I lost one eye and both of my outer ears. I used to stare at myself in the mirror because I was so good looking and now I can't stand to look at myself. To add insult to injury I will spend the rest of my life behind bars.

WORKING ADDICT

Crack head, junkie, dope addict you name it I've been called that and much worse. I of course don't see it that way at least not in the beginning. I called it a social habit but not an addiction. Never once did I ask or beg anyone for anything. I prided myself on being able to hold my own. Without anyone's help I got a good job, nice home, fly gear and all the paid cuties were checking for me. I had it going on and I knew it. So what if I smoked a little on weekends, holidays and the occasional party. What I did with the money I worked so hard for was nobody's business but my own.

The life I lead as a child was not a happy one. I've seen all the promising people in my family get sucked down the drug addiction drain. My father sold heroin and stashed it in our home. My mother was young and curious so one day when she was home alone she tried it. Needless to say two years later she died of an over dose in the bathroom. Both my father and brother were killed in a shoot out one protecting the other. I experienced all of these tragedies in my life before the age of seventeen. So when I look back on my life especially where I came from, I swore to myself that I would never get hooked because my eyes have seen the destruction of drugs.

I was able to keep my word until I met and fell in love with Devon. Now that was an addiction. He was a famous foot ball player. Light brown eyes; skin the color of ebony smooth and rich. He stood six feet tall two inches with broad shoulders that I could hold on to and a strong muscular body. He kept his head clean shaven and he smelled like heaven. Now this brotha was fine as hell and he got it going on. I knew he would be my first and last love. No one had the power to make me feel the way he did. When I was with him I felt on top of the world. He treated me like royalty. We went everywhere together. He opened my eyes to a whole new world.

Traveling to different islands, cultural events he even spoke two other languages. I was hopeless, following him around like a love sick puppy.

His favorite thing to do was party. We partied in every city. It was becoming increasingly difficult to hang with him and work. When I brought it to his attention he put a ring on my finger and said, "I can take care of you, you won't want for anything." Physically, financially, emotionally, spiritually... I got you.

Besides, no wife of mine will have to work a nine to five. So I quit my job, gave up my place and moved in with him. I was so in love, marrying the man of my dreams. I couldn't be happier. We partied and drank all night every night and slept during the day.

One night we were hanging out in his favorite club in Cali and one of his friends came in with some new shit. Devon's motto was he'll try anything once. I never really worried about him getting hooked on anything because he had his head on straight. To make a long story short he tried it and loved it. The next time we were in Cali his friend was right there with the same stuff. This time Devon asked me to join him and since nothing happened to him the first time he took it I joined him. It was unlike anything I've ever tried. It was very strong and very commanding. Devon started doing it more and more, he loved it. I on the other hand was afraid of it. I tried to stay clear of it because it had addicting qualities, I felt them. I didn't like losing control. Devon would get very angry when I refused to partake in his new favorite pass time. He would say things like I love you and I would never give you anything that would hurt you or I am your husband, don't you trust me? Eventually he wore me down and I gave into him. How could I continue to say no to those eyes and that body? I told myself that if I hadn't gotten addicted to anything by now that I was strong enough to beat anything.

Neither of us was.

We lost everything. The fancy houses, the beautiful clothes and his great money making career.

Everything up in smoke.

At first we were on the streets together staying here and there. That became increasingly difficult. It was too hard to hustle up enough money to support both of our food and drug habits so we went our separate ways.

My mother once said to me when she was high out of her mind on heroin, "as long as you got a pussy between your legs you'll always have money." So, on that note I decided to turn some tricks. At first the money was coming in good but then I came across some psychotic fuck that beat the shit out of me, burned me several times with a cigarette and left me for dead. Needless to say I stopped trickin. After I got out of the hospital and was half way to recovery I resorted to stealing because I wasn't strong enough to kick this thing on my own. One day after I copped my stuff I had a lot of nervous energy. I think that I may have gotten some bad shit because I couldn't keep still. So I told myself, "while your on the up and up better go on a stealing spree" so that's exactly what I did. I broke into this house that looked very expensive.

While I was filling up my nap sack with all the jewelry and money I could find I got hungry. I made my way to the kitchen and found some roast beef and an ice-cold beer in the fridge. I decided to get cocky and have myself a meal. Just as I finished stuffing my face I thought I heard a noise. I was scared shitless I just knew I was busted. Panic set in and I thought to myself what am I gonna do?!! The best place I could come up with was the bathroom. When I found it I jumped in the tub and pulled the shower curtain closed. As I laid flat in the tub I was so scared I was trembling. It was hard for me to be still but I did it. I managed to lay very still and very quiet so as not to give myself away. I listened and waited for the right time to make my escape. That time never came for me. I lay in that tub so very still listening so intently for something that wasn't there that I fell asleep. A very large Policeman woke me up as he cuffed my hands behind my back and hoisted me out of the tub. He turned to his partner as he escorted me to the car, "if this ain't the stupidest junkie we ever caught."

I'M INNOCENT

I AM I-N-N-O-C-E-N-T. I know, I know….when you get locked up everybody is "innocent" but I'm telling the truth and everybody else is full of shit. Let me plead my case to you.

My name is Ray and I'm only twenty years old. Fucked up is the name of my life story. I had a dark cloud over my head before I was born. Let me explain… I was born with multiple disabilities. A wheelchair is my mode of transportation because I was born without legs. They never developed passed the knee. As if that wasn't bad enough one of my arms didn't develop pass the elbow. I can't even take a shit like a normal man. I have to go in a bag through a hole in my stomach. I owe all this to my wonderful parents who cared enough about me to do drugs together while my mom was pregnant with me.

It's not all bad. I do have artificial limbs but just like everything else in my life they serve no purpose because they don't fit. Since my wheelchair is not electric I guess I'll continue to push myself around with the one good arm that I have.

Somebody please tell me how the hell am I suppose to survive in jail? I can't even protect myself. A walking...well a rolling target for every abuse known to man is what I'll be. I'm not afraid to admit that I'm scared shitless.

Three days ago I was sitting on the corner beggin for money from people who passed by. I was having a good day, just a little passed two and I already made a hundred dollars. Something told me that this day was too good to be true. Next thing I know cops ran up on me knocked me out of my chair and to the ground. One of them yelled shut up and don't move like I had a damn choice. I had no idea what was going on or why I was being harassed. I know pan handling is frowned upon but they didn't have to be so fucking brutal. I wasn't stealing. I thought to myself I'm definitely going to make a complaint as soon as I get the chance.

After being up for more than twenty four hours and going thru the system I finally got to see a judge. That's when I found out what I was being arrested for.

I was being accused of assault and battery with a bat. I lost it. I couldn't believe this shit. I started yelling at the judge. "You have got to be fucking stupid!" Are you blind or just that fucking stupid!! I can't assault or batter anybody with a bat if I wanted to you stupid prick. For that outburst he added ninety more days to my already unjustified sentence.

OUT OF THE PAN AND INTO THE FIRE

Our father who are in heaven our Lord be thy name...

If you can hear me dear lord, please get me out of this hell that is my life. Praying is something I did every chance I got since I married Paul.

When I met Paul he had the kindest soul. He was such a gentle man. We dated a year then we married on a small tropical island under a beautiful sunset. After two weeks of living out our fantasies we returned home and settled into our lives together. It was a fairytale come true. He decided that he didn't want me to work so we could start on our family right away. Since I wanted kids too I didn't see a problem. It was beautiful at first but after a short period of time I started to see changes in him.

He would get irritated easily. Little things would make him very angry. He started having shouting outburst. At first I chalked it up to a bad day at the office and would dismiss it. The more I forgave the worse it got. It was at the point where I couldn't do anything right no matter how hard I tried. His harsh words became hard slaps then punches. He would never bruise my face only my body. After a fight he would always say, "See what you made me do?" Every fight happened so fast half the time I didn't even see it coming. I never even got the chance to get angry or defend myself. I went from being happy and in love to being terrified of this man who was supposed to be my husband. I didn't know what to do or where to turn. I was scared for my life.

One day I looked in the mirror and I didn't recognize myself. I saw a shell of the woman I used to be. The woman staring back at me was withdrawn with dark circles around her eyes and permanent bruises on her skin. I didn't like what I saw or who I had become.

GET AWAY...was my only thought. I had to get away from him, my life depended on it. Going back home to my mama was my only choice. I had alienated the rest of my family and friends when I married Paul. Tuesdays are always the day Paul stays out late. That would be my escape day. Excitement started to build in me and I couldn't wait till Tuesday, just one more day! Freedom, it was so close I could taste it. I felt the old me coming back slowly. I thought it best to avoid confrontation at all cost. Told myself to be on my best behavior so I made a nice dinner, cleaned the house and myself up and did my hair and nails.

When I heard his car pull up I lit the candles for dinner and fixed our plates. To my relief he looked pleasantly surprised when he opened the door and saw what was waiting on him. I breathed a sigh of relief and thought we might even enjoy this dinner and time together. He came in washed up for dinner and without a word sat down across from me and started eating. Silence during the whole meal. Okay I thought if there's no talking then he can't get mad. I was wrong.

After he enjoyed his meal he sat back and sighed. Then his attention turned to me. He looked me up and down and was instantly enraged!!! He started ranting about me being all done up and how I must be cheating. He accused me of making a good meal to put him to sleep so that I could creep out with the next man. The more he talked the angrier he made himself. I started to get scared. I knew what was coming next so I got up slowly and started to back away from the table. "Baby..no I-I-I would never do" and before I could finish my sentence he slapped the shit out of me. He hit me right across the eye and jaw. I stumbled back and hit the back of my head on the kitchen counter. I felt the blood gush down the back of my head and neck. I cowered down to the floor into a ball with my arms up to protect my face and head. I begged in between sobs, "please no more...I'm sorr..." he kicked me in the ribs and I heard them crack. Oh the pain. I felt myself slipping; wanting to black out...I fought with myself to stay conscious. Breath I told myself BREATH. It was then I knew I would have to fight back or I would die that night. If you can hear me

Lord, help me I want to live. As I tried to get up he punched me in the face and I fell flat on the floor. He stood over me screaming. As he lifted his foot high off the floor to stomp on me I kicked him between his legs with strength I never knew I had. I became angry. Seeing red I lost control. I kicked him again and again. Punching, slapping and scratching him anywhere I could.

The last thing I remember was screaming no more NO MORE. When the cops arrived they found me covered in blood, mine and his. Sitting on the floor with a knife in my hand talking to a bloody mass that was Paul. "You promised to love and cherish me...it wasn't suppose to be like this...."

K.C.

I left by ambulance in handcuffs. He went out in a body bag. I had stabbed him twenty seven times.

NOT AGAIN

I can't believe I'm in this place again. I swore to myself that I would never return once I left.

The first time I was here I was just a boy living on the streets trying to figure out who I was. I had a good home once. My mom stayed home to raise me and my two brothers and sisters, five of us all together. I was the middle child. My dad wasn't around much. He was a preacher. That left mom home alone most of the time to raise us. I was kicked out of our "happy home" at the tender age of sixteen. My father came home one day unexpectedly and caught me experimenting with the boy that lived down the street. My pride wouldn't allow me to go home and beg to be taken back in. Being young and dumb I got mixed up with the wrong crowd. I kept in touch with the boy who lived down the street and he introduced me to drugs and all kinds of kinky sex. I did shit the wildest bunch couldn't imagine just to survive. The key word is survive…and that I did. I got locked up for prostitution when I was seventeen. I made myself a promise to get my life together. I knew that if I didn't I would die on those streets.

Although I was on my own at an early age I was brought up with good strong values. It was time to put them to use. Since I was still considered a minor I was sent to juvie. While there I attended school and got my G.E.D. since I was good with my hands I took a computer course. By the end of the class I received a certificate and the knowledge of putting together and taking apart any computer. I also learned how to install and delete any program on the market. I can also type a hundred words a minute. By the time I was released from juvie I had a great job a nice apartment, some money saved up and a good man.

Scratch that, amazing man.

I met him on the Internet. We became pen pals and fell in love. He said he would wait for me. He's the one that got me the job at the prevention center teaching computers to America's "lost" youth. I don't know why they call us that. I never considered myself lost, just gay. Maybe a little confused in the beginning but I got it together now.

I went into juvie as George and came out as Glorious. I let my hair and nails grow long then I found me an M.D. on the street and he gave me female hormones. Now I have full round breast most women would kill for. If I may toot my own horn for a second, Glorious is definitely gorgeous. I keep my hair and nails tight and I dress something fierce. After about a year of being able to stand on my own feet SAM proposed to me and of course I said yes. I couldn't believe how nicely my life was coming together. Finally I had no complaints. For the first time that I can remember being truly happy and satisfied.

Early one Saturday morning I was called into work. Any other time I would have been happy to do it but this particular morning I just didn't want to go. I should've followed my first mind but they pushed and I gave in like I always do when it's for the kids. My heart and soul goes out to those kids because we share a common bond. I've been where they are and I'm living proof that this too shall pass. (No matter the problem)

I was dressed and heading for the train at seven a.m.

A block from the train this drunken fool comes out of nowhere and tries to kick it to me. He tried to grab my hand and missed. Then he says "hey ma can I holla at you fo a minute?" I ain't got time for you right now, I'm late for work. I knew he was nothing but trouble. He reeked of liquor and weed. I kicked up my pace hoping he would go away or pass out. No such luck. The more I ignored him the more aggressive he became. When he touched my hair, girrrl...you know that was the last straw. I had to let my inner man out. I stopped dead in my tracks, turned around and looked him dead in his grill. In my deepest voice I said "nigga you needs to step! I'm more of a man than you'll ever be and I know you can't handle this." You should have seen the stunned look on his face.

K.C.

That shit was funny as hell. I walked away laughing my ass off leaving him standing there with his mouth open. I got about ten feet away when he started yelling and threatening me. Said he was gonna kick my ass. I told you to step I yelled back without breaking my stride. When he realized that I wasn't going to stop and entertain him he threw his bottle of Cisco. What was left of it spilled out all over my hair and clothes before it hit the ground and shattered in front of me. Now I was pissed off to the highest of pisstivity. "OH NO YOU DIDN'T!" This mother fucker must have lost his mind. He ran up to me, swung and busted my lip when I tasted my own blood I completely lost it. First my hair and clothes and then my face. I felt my lip start to swell. "You got the right one baby!" I yelled as I kicked off my heels. I beat him down like he stole something. By the time the cops came he had a busted lip two black eyes and a gash in his forehead.

We both got locked up. The cops laughed their asses off at the brotha for trying to write a check that his ass couldn't cash.

STOLEN INNOCENSE

My story is told from a different perspective. Although I'm not behind bars I am in prison. It's a mental prison, held captive by my own mind.

I was born and raised for the most part in Mexico to Maria and Juan Santos. I am the second oldest of seven children. Growing up we were poor. It was difficult not knowing when or where our next meal was coming from especially when all around us people from other countries came to our home and got the best our country had to offer. They came for food, fun, rest and relaxation. They were catered to and it was usually at the expense of us Mexicans.

The resorts that everyone from afar came to enjoy were built on the backs of my relatives. For their hard work, blood, sweat and tears they were paid pennies. It seemed like the richer the resorts got the poorer we became.

The men weren't the only ones who worked. We all had to pitch in and do our part. Some of the women and most of the children in my town worked at night. While the woman solicited drunken vacationers looking for a good time the children sold friendship bracelets that they made during the day.

It wasn't customary for the children to stay in school. From birth to age three you stayed at home with your abuela (grandmother) and she taught you the basics. From age three to six you went to work and sold friendship bracelets. From age six to eleven you attended school. At the age of eleven if you were a boy you went to work with your father, learned a trade and were paid for your assistance. If you were a girl that was pretty and built a certain way you were put into training until you turned twelve. We were trained how to please a man to perfection by our fathers or uncles. It was customary that your father or uncle took your virginity. In my case it was my father.

At first sex was very painful for me but after the first month I got used to it. I got lessons three times a week at night from my popi. During the day I got lessons from my mami on personal hygiene and protection. She taught me so much and I soaked it all up like a sponge. I learned the art of massage and masturbation. She even made me do a certain exercise that kept me tight called kegel; I did those all day everyday.

As a child I looked up to my popi. He also taught me a lot. The first thing he taught me was not to be rigid. He used to always say "no one wants a rigid lover." He taught me rhythm and how to keep his pace. I learned to match him stroke for stroke fast or slow. After mastering that I was taught oral sex. That was more difficult for me.

I kept gagging and even threw up a couple of times. My popi was worried that I wouldn't get the hang of it. He said that I really needed to know how to do this well because it was the biggest moneymaker. He said that foreign men loved to get their dick sucked and paid good money for it because they couldn't get their women to do it.

I was so worried about disappointing my popi I didn't know what to do. I told my mami of my troubles and she gave me some fruit flavored spray that numbed my mouth and throat. I went back to my popi the following night after using the spray.

Without saying a word I handed him a cold beer then undressed him from the waist down. I started to suck him slow and long the way he taught me. When he got hard he took over our rhythm and speed. I matched his every movement with my mouth being careful not to use my teeth. When he started to buck the way he said most men did right before they came, I grabbed his ass and squeezed pulling him into me. He grabbed my hair and let out a groan as he exploded. I smiled to myself because I knew that I had made my popi proud.

The first lesson of the following week was my last and most difficult phase of becoming what my father called his perfect little "mejer de la noche" (woman of the night.)

I thought I would die the first time I had anal sex. I prayed that once I passed this part no one would ever request this of me. No amount of money would be worth it. I bled more from my ass than I did from my pussy when I lost my virginity. My popi kept stroking my head and telling me to relax but I just couldn't. He got so frustrated with me that he stormed away leaving me on the bed crying. I had failed him and that feeling was worse than the act itself. That night after everyone went to sleep my mami came to me and told me not to worry that she would help me get thru this just as before. She kissed me on the forehead and said "Del sol me, miha." (Go to sleep my little one.)

The next day after everyone had gone my mami woke me up and fed me. After that she bathed me then massaged me until every muscle in my body was completely relaxed. She gave me a spray that was similar to the one I used on my throat except it had a very slippery feeling to it. She also gave me a weird looking device. She looked into my eyes and asked me if I remembered when I learned to masturbate? "Yes mami I do." Well it's the same thing except from the back. Instead of your fingers use this tool. Now practice and with that she left closing the door behind her. I sat there for a moment trying to relax myself and then I did as I was told.

I used the oily spray on my back door until it

felt tingly and numb. The hardest part was inserting the round knob looking part. Once that was in the rest was easy. I worked it in and out until I could take the whole thing. I couldn't wait to show popi.

The following week I would make twelve and that marked the end of my training-practice sessions with my popi. It was kind of a bittersweet transaction. I would miss my popi but now I could start to bring in some money to help my family. I was nervous, scared and excited all at the same time. My Madre took me shopping for make up, body spray, shoes and clothes. I got my hair and nails done. The preparations for my first night of work made me feel like a queen. The last night of my childhood I was fed my favorite meal of arroz con pollo y plantanos. That night I slept soundly.

As I prepared for my first night of work my Madre came in and told me not to worry because it was carnival time. Everyone did well because of all the vacationers looking for a good time.

When the van came to round up the women and children my popi kissed me on the head and told me that I was already the best mujer de la noche of my piers because I had the best trainer. "I know you will make me proud." With that said I was out the door.

The van driver took us to a dark alley right off the main hotel strip. The mothers blocked off the entrance so we would be protected from the police. They also watched the younger kids while they ran threw the crowded street selling their bracelets. The van driver lined us up at the back of the alley then went to round up some men for us. He also collected the money up front to ensure that we didn't get ripped off. Each girl had an envelope that the driver held onto until the end of the night. During our shift whatever money we made was put into our envelope. He got his ten percent right off the top and the girls got to pocket whatever tips they may have gotten after there performance.

There were eight of us that started together that night. They called us newbies. I looked at the other girls and could tell that they were scared and nervous. One girl even threw up. I knew I didn't have anything to worry about after that episode. A half hour went by before the van driver came back with two guys. He shined a light on us and told them to pick whom they wanted. I was the first picked. A girl named Cherry was the next one up and I could tell she would be my competition because she was just as ambitious as I was. I'm sure she was striving to please her popi, just as I was.

The guy that wanted me was young, strong looking and handsome. I could sense he was a little nervous. The van driver whispered in my ear "go easy on him, he's a virgin." I smiled to myself and thought, "This should be easy. If I mess up he won't know because he's never done this before. I liked the idea of being someone's teacher." I took him by the hand and led him deeper into the alley. When we reached the couch I turned to face him. Remembering what my mami said "never kiss a paying customer in the mouth" so I started with his ear. Breathing softly from my mouth into his ear then licking around the outer part before taking his lobe into my mouth and sucking on it. All this time I was still holding his hands, a little trick I taught myself. Holding onto his hand lets me know if he's pleased with me. He was, so I pressed my body to his and put one of his hands on my ass. I took my free hand and placed it on his ass so that I could show him what to do. I ventured to his neck using my tongue to softly lick and strongly suck on him. This made his dick rock hard. That meant he was ready for me to mount him. I pulled away from him long enough to pull his pants down. I nudged him down to the couch. He was quite large, not like popi at all. I reach inside my pouch and pulled out my oil and a condom for him. I rolled the condom down his shaft with my mouth then oiled myself. I secured the condom with my hand before climbing on top of him, slowly inserting him inside of me. Because he was so big and I was so tight I could feel him throbbing as I eased him in and out. His breathing started to get louder and faster. Once I got him all the way in I increased my speed to match his panting. He grabbed my hips and pushed himself deeper into me with each thrust. I felt that we were nearing the end so I squeezed his dick with my pussy muscles. He said in a deep guttural voice "I dios mio, I me voy a venire!" (Oh my God I'm Cuming!)

I received my first tip of five American dollars. I was glad that my first customer was with a fellow Mexican, even if he wasn't born and raised in Mexico.

This went on for about two years. I became the top mujer de la noche because I was the most requested so I made the most money and tips. My parents were so proud they bragged to anyone who would listen. It got so bad that the other girls grew to hate me, all except Cherry. She was still my best competition. We actually became friends.

My brother and uncles started looking at me with lust. They felt that if strangers could have me they should too. My popi wouldn't allow it. He said it wasn't moral. They didn't like it but they stayed away from me because they feared my popi.

One evening while I was getting ready for work my brother and the van driver brought my popi home late from work. They had taken him to the local bar and gotten him so drunk that he was incoherent. They had to carry him into the house. When they put him down he started vomiting. It was so bad that my mami was worried. The van driver told her not to worry "stay home and take care of him and the little ones and your son and I will look after the girls while they work." she smiled and was grateful for the help.

That night when I left I felt so uneasy. The guys in the front reeked of liquor. There were only two other girls in the van that night and they were whispering to each other and giving me dirty looks. I questioned the driver about the other five girls when I realized he had bypassed their homes. My brother told me to shut up and mind my business in the nastiest tone. My heart started to race when we turned down a road that led away from the main strip and towards a deserted beach. Uh-uh-uh this is not the right way! Where are you taking us! No one said a word. I started to panic: I knew I was all alone when I asked the other girls if they knew what was going on and they replied in unison "shut up bitch!" the van slowed down then came to a stop on the dark deserted beach. I said a silent prayer then got up and tried to escape. When I darted towards the door the locks slammed shut on all the doors. The driver turned the ignition off and the music up. My brother and the van driver got undressed while the girls were slapping me around in the back. When the guys were ready each girl grabbed an arm and held it above my head. Through my screams I heard my brother say, family first! He was drunk and muttering something about my golden pussy. I begged him "padamiso" don't do this to me! No one had ever entered me raw not even popi. My brother was intent on doing so. Just as he grabbed his dick to guide it into me I kicked him with the heel of my shoe and it made a deep gash in his leg. That just made him mad. "Oh so you like it rough, no problem." He picked me up with one hand while he lay on the floor of the van. He put me on top and rammed his dick into me. He held me firmly in place by the waist so I couldn't get away. The girls moved quickly to help the men get me under control. One girl stood over my brother's head and grabbed my arms. She tied them together and pulled me flat on top of my brother. At the same time the van driver and the other girl spread my legs and tied them to each side of the van I never felt so helpless in all my life. I stopped fighting and screaming and gave up when I realized it was useless.

When the men realized they had the situation under control they let the girls restrain me so they could concentrate on the crime they were intent on committing.

My brother started to work himself in and out while the van driver tried to enter me from behind. I thought I was off the hook because I was so dry and so tight that he tore the skin on the head of his dick trying to get in. he let out a howl and I prayed that he would back off but my prayers went unanswered. He made the girls spread my ass apart while he licked it. He did that until I was sopping wet with his spit. Then he mounted me again this time slowly as to not injure himself. Never once did my brother stop what he was doing. I couldn't scream if I wanted to because one of the girls had stuffed a rag into my mouth. At that moment the driver penetrated me and I let out a muffled scream. I looked into my brother's face and pleaded for help with my eyes but he was in another place. I looked at the girls and they looked away. All I could do was cry.

The men developed a rhythm, one in one out, one in one out. This went on for what seemed like hours. As I slipped in and out of consciousness I prayed for it to come to and end and finally it did. They exploded simultaneously.

Before they untied me my brother threatened me. The look in his eyes told me that he would follow thru with his threats.

I kept quiet for fear of my life. It took me about four months to come to terms with what went down and start to move on. Just as I started to heal mentally I got sick physically. I couldn't keep any food down. I had a hard time staying awake and I ached all over. My parents thought I had some kind of stomach virus so they took me to the hospital.

We found out that I was pregnant. They took me home and beat me until I told them of that dreadful night. I told them everything in detail. They were mortified and popi was outraged. Crying, my popi fell to his knees and begged my forgiveness. "How could I have let this happen to my precious princess? I am so sorry."

Don't worry meja we will fix this my mami cried. My brother had disgraced the family. My parents sat and thought for a while about how to rectify the situation. They didn't want this to get out and bring further shame upon the family so they decided to take me to the clinic to get rid of it. It was there that we found out that I was to far along to get an abortion. That was a sad day for my parents.

My mami started to panic so my popi flew us to Los Angeles to take care of it. Someone told him that the rules were different there. They gave him the name to a doctor that could help us. The trip cost us our life savings. When we arrived in Los Angeles we had no trouble finding the doctor. He said he would help but he was curious as to how someone so young ended up pregnant. For some reason my father felt the need to oblige this fellow Mexican M.D. He blurted out our life story to this stranger. When popi finished he sighed with relief, glad to be able to share his burden.

We all looked up at the doctor's face, his mouth was open and he wore a horrified look upon it. I knew it wasn't a good idea to enlighten him but since this whole thing came out no one would listen to me. He couldn't believe that someone would steal a child's innocence let alone his own child. He immediately called the cops. I was taken into protective custody, ripped away from my family. My parents and brother were taken to central booking. Everything happened so fast.

There I was in a strange place scared alone and confused. I was placed in a small group home. They started psychotherapy on me immediately. The more therapy they gave me the more confused and messed up I became. I didn't know what was right or wrong anymore, all I wanted was to go home with my family.

Everybody asked me questions while my questions went unanswered. Feeling defeated I just retreated into myself. I shut down and stopped talking all together. Afraid that I would hurt myself or someone else they put me in a mental institution.

The hospital kept me so drugged up, half the time I didn't know who or where I was.

The matter of the pregnancy was never

resolved. I was caught up in so much red tape that the procedure was never done. My body went through so many physical changes my mind couldn't keep up. Not one of the many doctors I saw on a daily basis took the time to explain what was happening to me.

Giving birth was the worst. I had no idea what was happening when I went into labor. When the pains started coming and wouldn't stop, I screamed and banged on my cell door until I heard running footsteps. They came, put me on a stretcher and shipped me to another floor. By the time they got me in stirrups and someone took a look I heard them yell between my screams "she's crowning!" no one had to tell me to push. I did it involuntarily. Four good pushes and out she came, nine pounds seven ounces. I thank God I was blessed with a quick labor and delivery. She was the most beautiful baby I had ever seen. I spoke my first words since I entered the institute. "Puedo awonta la nina?" (Can I hold my baby?) A light went on some where inside of me and I knew I wanted to keep her. They cleaned her up and let me hold her while they cleaned me up.

I named her Fa-mel-lia because she was the only family I had left. No one ever told me what became of my parents or my brother. At least I know that my younger siblings are well cared for because we left them in Mexico with my grandmother and aunt. I was talking to my daughter when the doctors came and took her from me. I didn't understand. They were talking amongst themselves, treating me as if I wasn't there. I heard someone say something about unstable and ward of the state. It was all a jumble. A nurse left the room with my baby and I started freaking out. I started to cry, screaming and yelling for my baby. "Dame la nina, por favor... dame la nina!" I became hysterical. The staff constricted me and someone stuck me with a needle that knocked me out almost instantly. When I came to I was back in my room staring at those same four walls. No baby and no family, I was all alone again. In between sobs all I could think about was "what did I do in my life that was so bad to deserve the karma that was biting me so hard."

BOOTY BANDITS

A bad ass kid was what I was since I could walk and talk. I was always into something. No matter how much trouble I got into I didn't deserve the punishment I received.

Going to jail didn't phase me and how I ended up there is not important. It's what happened to me while I was in jail that changed my life.

In jail they don't allow you to wear certain colors because they are symbolic to gangs. Just because they take away the colors of the gangs doesn't mean they don't exist. **THEY DO.** I've learned that if you want to survive in there you better get in one. There is protection in numbers.

Me, I had a chip on my shoulder and in the outside world I never needed anybody. So when I got locked down I took my chip and my attitude with me. Told every man who approached me to fuck off. Refusing to join any gang, I thought I was a one man army. So instead of doing something or somebody to prove my loyalty I was the proof of somebody else's loyalty.

Working in the laundry department didn't allow me to spend much time with the G.P. the only thing I got to do with the general population was eat. My shower time was later than usual so I'm not heavily guarded by the

CO's. There is always a guard but this particular night in the middle of my shower after I soaped up my face and head the guard yelled that he'd be right back. I didn't think nothing of it. As I turned to face the running water to rinse off I was brutally attacked.

Someone hit me across the back of my knees with a hard object which caused me to buckle. Hitting my head on the shower wall on my way down, my eyes filled with blood and soap. I couldn't see. All I knew was that I was out numbered by two. Being the bad ass that I was there was no fucking way I was going down without a fight. I heard one say "let us know when you hear somebody coming." As I hit the floor on all four's the one behind me tried to mount me like

K.C.

a dog in heat. When he paused to unbuckle and drop his pants I kicked him in his balls and he dropped screaming like a bitch. Buying myself some time I tired to wipe the blood and soap out of my eyes so I could see my attackers. Just when I thought the coast was clear somebody kneed me in the nose. More blood gushed out of my face. That blow put me in a daze. Another guy took advantage of my state and shoved his dick into my mouth. When he hit the back of my throat with his dick it caused me to gag and brought me back to realty. When I realized I was losing this war I bit down as hard as I could only letting go when the blood started spurting out. When I let go the guy fell to the floor and passed out. At that point I thought I had won and the war was over.

In much pain, I struggled to a standing position rinsed myself clean head to toe. As I turned to leave I was hit again with the same hard object in the head. I was slipping, how could I forget about that third guy?? He had an advantage over me he hit me again and again and again until I couldn't move if I wanted to. When he paused to undo his pants I tried to turn over onto my back but I couldn't move my legs...they were broken... Needles to say I lost that war and everything else when he succeeded at raping me.

WHAT I WOULDN'T DO

This is how I know what love is: Jesus Christ laid down his life for us.

I would do the same for my family.

I know what I did was wrong but I did it for all the right reasons...

So much has gone wrong in my life I don't know where to begin my story. I guess I can start by saying that I've never been in trouble with the law until now.

K.C.

I'm not gonna give you a sob story about how society screwed me up. Yeah, I had it hard growing up but I had a plan and I knew I was gonna make it. You ever wanted something so bad you could taste it? That's how I felt about climbing out of the ghetto. I wanted to succeed so bad I could taste it. I did alright for myself as long as I was by myself. I almost made it but I got sidetracked by love.

Her name is Sasha. She was the most beautiful girl I had ever laid eyes on. Half Asian and half black with skin so soft and smooth... the color of dark chocolate. Her hair was the color of ebony long thick and shiny like a black stallions Maine. Her frame, petite and well per portioned. What I loved most about her where her eyes. They were slanted like her mother's jet black like her hair and deep as the ocean. They made her look so exotic. She was a perfect ten in my book. She had everything. Looks, brains and a sweet and caring personality to sweeten the pot. I fell in love with her almost instantly. I felt she deserved the moon and the stars and I wanted to be the one who gave it to her. The two of us became an item and together we decided to climb. She made me want to do better and I did the same for her so we got an apartment together. We both worked and tried to save money in between paying the bills. The little bit we put away from every check started to add up and it finally looked like we would get out in just a few more years.

Just as our lives seemed to be on a stable track our road took a turn for the worse. The company I worked for was about to go belly up unless they downsized. You know how the saying goes the last to be hired is always the first to be fired. Unfortunately I was amongst that group. Along with my great job went my benefits. At first I didn't worry too much because we had a little money saved. The very next day I hit the pavement looking for another job. What I thought would be a quick and easy task turned into a long drawn out process. Five months past still no job and our money was running out.

One night Sasha sat me down with tears in her eyes. She looked deep into my eyes and said "we need to talk, I've been trying to wait for a good time to tell you but my time has run out. I know this is not the best of times but you need to know." I thought she was dying. Baby, are you sick? No nothing like that. Then spit it out cause you're scaring me. She took a deep breath and a long pause then said "I'm pregnant." I was dumbfounded by her news. Before I could say anything she said "I wanted to surprise you with this news but on that very same day you lost your job. I didn't want to overwhelm you so I decided to wait until you found another job but that was five months ago. If I didn't tell you soon you sure would have noticed on your own." I was filled with so many different emotions I didn't know which one to release first. After my initial shock wore off I blurted out ... you've been keeping this from me for five months... how could you! She lowered her eyes and her voice and said six months. WHAT! I was so hurt. I thought we shared everything? Why...? Baby, I'm sorry my intention wasn't to hurt you. I just didn't want to burden you with more stress. I've seen how bummed out you've been since you lost your job and it's just getting worse. How could you possibly think that? Don't you know how much I love you? The look in her eyes told me that she had some doubts. You make me want to be a better man, I thrive because of you. I grabbed her and held her tight. As we cried together I thought about how I've been so stressed out about finding a job that I hadn't even noticed the changes in her body. I stepped back and took a good look at her. Her face was a little fuller. Her breasts were definitely at least two sizes larger. I knelt down so I could be at eye level with her belly which was still kind of flat with a bulge at the bottom. I touched her there and it was firm. She pressed her hands on top of mine and knelt down so that she could look into my eyes. "Please know that I never meant to hurt you. Then she gave me the most passionate kiss and all was forgiven. At that moment our child moved under our joined touch. I pulled back from her kiss with a gasp... BABY!! Did you feel that!! Of course silly. I vowed to myself to get back on my feet before the little one arrived.

Time passed quickly and my son was born. Watching him come into this world gave me a new found respect to all women who have given birth. Sadly to say, things didn't get any better. They steadily got worse. She even applied for welfare but they turned her down because she had been working and she had a little savings. Each day I applied for work and was turned down it took away a piece of my manhood.

One day I came home from an all day job hunt startled because Sasha and the baby were both crying. Baby what's wrong, why are you guys crying. He's been crying all day because he's hungry. So why haven't you given him the breast, are your nipples still sore? That's not it. Then what's the problem? I can't make milk because I haven't had any thing to eat in two days. Why aren't you eating? She immediately got angry. Where is your head? Are you delirious from hunger yourself? Haven't you noticed that there's no more money in the bank, I'm not working and there hasn't been any food in the fridge in days.

I can't eat what we don't have. Damn, I'm sorry I hadn't noticed. (I hadn't noticed because I eat when I'm on interviews. Most places offer you juice, coffee, donuts, sandwiches and things like that. Every place I go I eat something but I wasn't about to tell her that, not now.) Don't worry I'll fix it and with that I went out the door. I didn't know what to do. I had no one I could turn to for help. For the first two hours I walked around collecting bottles which only got me four dollars which wasn't enough to get a can of formula or a decent meal for Sasha. I sat on the curb trying to figure out what the fuck I was gonna do. I sat on that curb for hours. When I couldn't come up with anything else I prayed to God and asked him for forgiveness for what I was about to do. "Dear Lord, you know that I'm just trying to feed my family"

Looking around, the streets were empty and so was the bodega on the corner. I went in nonchalantly and proceeded to take a case of formula. After it was securely hidden in my jacket I walked slowly towards the front door. Just as I walked passed the register I heard a clicking sound that stopped me dead in my tracks. The owner said with such disgust in his voice "I HATE YOU! ALL YOU BLACK MOTHERFUCKERS ARE JUST ALIKE. You think you can come in here night after night take what you want and I have to pay for it! Well tonight you will pay my friend. You will pay dearly. Before I could say anything in my defense he shot me twice, once in each knee. I fell to the floor in great agony. Before I passed out the owner picked up the phone... I heard him say in a frantic voice "operator, there is an intruder in my store he's been harassing me for weeks today he has attacked me please send help fast I fear for my life." After he hung up he said "pay backs a bitch!"

My name is James. I'm a twenty four year old black man telling my story from a jail house hospital bed. The worse part of my punishment is not that I'm in prison but that I feel like I let my family down. I wasn't able to take care of them before I got locked up and I won't be able to take care of them when I get out because the doctors say that I'll never walk again.

LIFE LESSONS

When my time comes...may GOD have mercy on my soul.

I'm not in jail but I feel like I should be.

My name is Wanda and I'm a single mother of four boys living in Harlem. That's right four boys, so you can imagine how hard things have been.

I was married once. I married my first love right out of high school. We lived with his mother until we got pregnant with our first son. While he worked I applied for whatever city help I could get. We were approved for section eight. So with that we moved into our very first apartment in the projects. In the beginning we were so happy and very much in love. When the baby turned four months I got a job to help out and his mother kept little Carl while we worked. Just as we were settling into our life and routine I got pregnant again. We knew it was gonna be hard raising two kids still being kids our selves but not impossible. So we buckled down. I worked all the way until the end of my pregnancy. The job gave me a baby shower on my last day of work. The very next day I went into labor. Twelve hours later Kevin was born. Our boys were eighteen months apart. I never thought having two babies in pampers would be so hard. Those boys gave us a run for our money. They were always into something. Sleep is a whole other issue. I haven't slept thru the night in two years. Carl started keeping me up at night in the womb. Now that Kevin is here they have a tag team method. One wakes up and when he goes back to sleep the other one wakes up. By the time everyone is sleep at the same time it's time for me to get up and start with my daily routine. My husband and I decided that I should go on birth control since he was against abortion. Finally after a year we were back on a steady routine that the kids learned to follow.

K.C.

I went back to work and things didn't seem so bad. My husband and I actually were able to spend some quality time together. For a while we were so stressed out I didn't think we were gonna make it.

Some time had passed and the boys were four and five and in school. Thank God for school. No more baby sitting fees or diapers. I was able to go back to school myself and get a better job. Things were good.

Why is it that whenever people let their guards down life hits you hard and knocks the wind out of you? Most folks are usually left looking dumbfounded trying to figure out what the hell just happened.

To make a long story short, my husband and I were happy virtually problem and stress free. The sex was so good between us we couldn't seem to get enough of one another. You would have thought we were rabbits, everyday sometimes twice. As they say, all good things must come to an end, and it was good. To good to be without consequences.

I was Pregnant again, this time with twins. I guess the pill wasn't strong enough. When I found out all I could do was cry. I was scared to tell my husband for he would pack up and leave. I finally mustard up the strength to tell him. He handled it rather well.

After Chris and Kyle were born thirty minutes apart I got my tubes tide. I always thought that having twins were special until I had my own. I have to admit they were the cutest little things you ever did see. When I brought them home all they did was sleep shit and spit up. They were Carl and Kevin reincarnated to the fifth power.

When Chris and Kyle hit the terrible two's my husband hit the streets running. He went out for pampers and wipes one day and never came back. He left me alone to raise four boys by myself. At first I was worried sick that something happened to him. Two days later I came home from the precinct to find he had been at the house and had taken all of his belongings. All he left was a letter stating that he couldn't handle being here any longer.

All this time I thought we were in this together. How the hell did he think I felt? Especially since I was the one in close contact with the kids all of the time. He helped out once in a while when he felt like it. We both worked hard but I was the primary care taker of the house and kids. I thought in doing that it would make things easier on him but I guess I was wrong. If it was hard for us to do it together how the hell did he think I was gonna do it alone? I was hurt for a long time behind him leaving especially the way he left. After the hurt was gone I became very bitter and my boys suffered the brunt of it. My boys missed there father growing up.

K.C.

They tried to reach out to him on several occasions but he never responded. I did the best I could by them. What I couldn't provide they got from the streets. I fought long and hard to keep them from the streets but I was fighting a loosing battle.

By the time Carl and Kevin were grown they had been in and out of jail a number of times. Their two little brothers were trying to follow in their foot steps. Chris is the only one who hasn't been in any trouble with the law. The first time Kyle got in trouble I was at my wits end. He wouldn't listen to me and I was out of ideas on how to keep him on the straight and narrow.

I got a call while I was at work from a truant officer stating that my son Kyle had been picked up for cutting school and getting caught steeling from the local convenience store. They told me in order for him to be released with just a warning I had to go get him. I had to beg my boss not to fire me for leaving early yet again. By the time I reached the court house I was mentally and physically drained. I just wanted to get my son and go home. When they led me to the cell he was being held in I saw him laughing and cracking jokes with the other fools. I was furious. I didn't know what I was gonna do. He had to be taught a lesson in order to save his life.

I went in spoke to the judge and explained my situation. We came up with a scared straight plan. I decided to let them process him. I figured four days in jail should straighten him out. The judge agreed and off Kyle went. I cried and prayed for my baby because I knew he was scared but drastic time's calls for drastic measures. I didn't want him to end up like his older brothers. The last thing I said to him was you have to be taught a lesson, this is for your own good. It's the only way I know how to save your life. Just know that I love you. Your brother and I will be waiting for you when you get out. Hopefully you'll be ready to turn over a new leaf. With that said he was whisked away on a bus full of hardened criminals headed for Connecticut. I called their father's mother because she was the only link I had to their father. Even though he hasn't been around he was still their father and I felt the need to inform him of the big things that happened in their lives. I told her what happened and she blew up at me screaming "what kind of mother are you?! How could you do such a thing to your own flesh and blood? If any thing happens to him I'll never forgive you!" by the time she finished laying me out I was a blubbering mess. After she said what she had to say she slammed the phone down in my ear.

Now I had doubts about the decision I had made for my son. Was she right? Was this punishment to harsh for my sixteen year old boy?

K.C.

On his third day I couldn't wait to get out of work so I could go home and get ready for my road trip to get my baby. By the time I had gotten home Chris was already ready to go. He had packed his brother some clean clothes, fried some chicken for the road and was waiting for me. Ma, can we leave now... I don't have a good feeling about this. The look in his eyes scared me. I've learned to trust his instincts when it came to his twin. What's wrong Chris? I've been feeling that he's been scared and anxious since he left but today it's a bit different, more intense... something is wrong. Why would he feel worse getting out then he did when he went in? I don't know but let me get a quick shower and throw on my driving clothes. We can go up early try to visit so we can see him our selves then camp out in the car till morning. Sounds like a plan. Ma, you do that and I'll get the music together for our ride. Don't forget my stand up comedy c.d. I showered and decided to wash my hair and mousse it so that when I rolled out of my car in the morning my short blonde curls would still look good. Chris and I secured the apartment so that Carl and Kevin couldn't get in and steal what little we had. I haven't seen either of them in about two weeks but they always seemed to know when the apartment was empty for a substantial amount of time. They've come here countless times and raided the fridge and cabinets, stolen the boys school clothes and sneakers. They've also taken my jewelry and any money left in the house. After a couple of times of this my younger boys and I got smart. I purchased an alarm system and we changed the locks and rigged the windows.

On the way up I studied Chris and I could tell that he was really worried. Don't worry Chris your brother is strong, he'll be okay. I hoped that he bought that because I didn't believe a word I had said. I was just as worried because when it came to his brother he was never wrong. I stepped on the gas once we hit the highway. Chris fell asleep half way thru our four hour road trip. As he slept I said a prayer for my twins which I did everyday. I didn't want them to end up like the other two.

The closer I got to Pred Tende Penitentiary the worse I felt. My stomach knotted up, my hands were cold and clammy and my head and neck were sweaty. I had two bouts of nausea that were so bad I had to pull over and get myself together. At that moment I knew in my gut that my baby was in trouble. I didn't know what it was but I knew it wasn't good. I floored it the rest of the way to the jail.

By the time I reached the visitors parking lot I was in full blown panic attack mode. I almost had a car accident trying to park the car. When my son realized what was happening to me he jumped up opened all the windows and calmed me down by stroking my hair and instructing me softly and calmly to relax and breath. I closed my eyes and concentrated on the sound of his voice. After about ten minutes my body obeyed, I was calm and back in control but I still couldn't shake the feeling in my gut. Chris grabbed his brother's clothes and we locked up the car. We ran all the way to the visitors building. After we were processed and cleared all the check points we were put on a bus and taken to the building where Kyle was being housed. As we were led into the building we saw an ambulance quickly approaching us. We shot each other a look that told me we were both thinking the same thing. We rushed to the front of the line to the window. We told the officer in unison "were here to see Kyle Black." What is your relationship to him? I'm his mother and I'm his brother. The officer radioed someone then waited. A response came over his speaker "bring them to the urgi med-lock exit ASAP!" That response brought instant tears to my eyes. Officer, what's happening? As we ran down the corridor he said "no time now for explanations ma'am. Your son is going out on emergency by way of paramedics. The ambulance is here for him already. Since he was due to go home in less than twenty-four hours you can ride with him if you like but we have to hurry. As we arrived at the exit they were coming down the other end of the hall with a stretcher and Kyle was on it. As they got closer I could see that he had been beaten very badly. His face was almost unrecognizable. I hated to think of what the rest of him looked like under that white sheet that was now being stained with his blood. "OH MY GOD…KYLE!" he responded to my voice Ma, you came. They put his stretcher right next to me so I could talk to him while they opened up and prepared the ambulance for him. I kissed his forehead tenderly of course I did. Chris is here too. I know…he's been with me since I got here. He has never left my side. It was silent for a moment then Kyle said I thought about what you said and I'm ready to turn over that leaf now mama. I've learned my lesson. I just want to make you proud. As they wheeled him to the entrance he said I'm just gonna take a little nap. Both Chris and I yelled NO! Kyle you can't go to sleep. Okay we only have room for one more so which one of you is going to ride with him? Chris looked at me with tears in his eyes, please let me ride with my brother. I couldn't bear to tell him no. Okay baby but you have to do everything in your power to keep him awake. When they closed the doors I knew that that would be the last time I saw my baby alive. The captain drove me to my car and I followed the ambulance to the hospital. When the ambulance pulled in and parked the paramedic who rode in the back with my boys got out and quietly closed the doors behind him. I got out of the car and ran towards the ambulance. As I got closer I could hear Chris's screams of agony coming from inside as he mourned for his brother. My grandmother used to call it the death cry. It was a distinct howl that could touch another's soul. When you heard it you knew instinctively that someone had died. I sank to my knees, buried my head in my hands and cried out... what have I done.

Epilogue

I put my semi-troublesome son in jail for a few days hoping it would scare some sense into him.

The officers put him in the wrong housing unit. They housed him with a gang but he wasn't in a gang. The gang members knew he didn't belong they thought he was from a rival gang so they beat him to death. All I wanted to do was teach him a lesson. I never thought in my wildest dreams that in three days of punishment my son would loose his life. For the rest of my life I have to live with the guilt of killing my son.

SEEK AND YOU SHALL FIND

If I ever learned anything worth teaching someone else it would be to follow your first instincts.

I think somewhere deep inside of me I knew I should have never married Rodney. We haven't been married long but we've been together for a life time. It was almost like love at first site, for me anyway. After everything we've been thru and all the years we spent together I still feel like he's not giving me his all. I've always felt like that. I should have quit while I was ahead. But instead of getting out I clung to him like he was God's gift to me. Every night I prayed that the love I felt for him would be returned to me. Slowly it was but not to the magnitude I felt it should be. I always felt like something wasn't right but I could never put my finger on it. So I chalked it up to being all in my head and let it go. Every now and again my inner turmoil would swell up in me and make me a little crazy. One side of my conscious told me "if he didn't love you he would have never married you." The other side said "look how long it took him maybe it was a marriage of convenience for him." I decided to stop picking and let things just be. We went on with our lives together but never really becoming one. Two years had past and things started to change between us. I thought as time past we were supposed to grow closer, we didn't. He started going out more. His hanging out late turned into all niters. God forbid I asked about his comings and goings he would fly off the handle or give me some lame excuse. I believed he was seeing another woman. Whenever I asked him if he was the answer was always no. I didn't believe him but I had nothing to go on but a haunch. Feeling defeated I let it go. I couldn't accuse him of something I had no proof of.

One night he came home at the crack of dawn. He was pissy drunk. He tried to get undressed and in the process of trying to get out of his pants he fell over and everything in his pocket came tumbling out. He didn't bother to get up, he fell asleep right there on the living room floor with his pants around his ankles and his shoes on. I had intended on helping him to bed but the contents from his pocket that had spilled out onto the floor were calling me. There was a pink slip of paper that looked like a receipt. I was hoping that it would give me some insight to where he had been. I opened up the paper and it was a receipt for a fourteen carat gold necklace with a diamond heart pendant. The date showed that he had purchased this a week before Valentines Day which was two months after my birthday so I knew he didn't buy it for me. I knew I wasn't crazy there was another woman. I made a copy of the receipt and put the original back where I found it. I was furious but I didn't act on it. With him I needed to be one hundred percent without a doubt or he would find a way to make me feel like it was all in my head. I was so angry I could have screamed but then I would have to explain my anger so instead I put his hand in a bowl of warm water and he peed on himself. I left him on the floor stinking of urine and went to bed.

Over the next two weeks I tried to find out what he was up to and who he was doing. I tried everything I could think of like getting into his phone but he kept it locked. I tried calling him while he was out to see if I could catch any back ground voices or noise that would give me any kind of clues but he never answered my calls when he was out. I had to face it I had no idea what I was doing so I hired a private detective to do the foot work for me. I set up a meeting with the D.T. and told him what I knew which wasn't much. All I knew for sure was that there was something going on and I needed to know what it was. He only asked me for a few things. The receipt with his credit card numbers on it his cell phone number the address to his job and of course a deposit of four hundred dollars. Two weeks later I received a phone call from the detective he had what I wanted we set up a meeting for the next day. I brought the remainder of four hundred dollars so I could get what I needed. That night I couldn't sleep at all. I couldn't wait to see pictures of the bitch he was creeping with. I was so mad my blood felt like it was boiling. There he was sleeping soundly without a care in the world. It was all I could do to keep from chocking the shit out of him in his sleep. Knowing for a fact that he had another woman I couldn't lay in the same bed with him. For the remainder of the night I laid on the couch staring at the ceiling thinking of ways to get my revenge. By sun up all I knew was somebody had an ass kicking coming big time and it wasn't gonna be me. By five thirty A.M. I was up and dressed in my workout gear. My appointment wasn't until noon and I had to find a way to get rid of all this pent up energy and anger. Sex would usually do it for me but today just the thought of sleeping with him made me sick to my stomach. I got down on my knees, held my hands high towards my heaven and I prayed "Dear God please shed some light on me, show me the way for right now I can not see clearly please fill my heart and soul with your peace and serenity Amen" I opened my eyes to find that I was crying. I felt so closed in I had to get out.

Out on the streets the sun was rising and the air was crisp, just the way I liked it. I took a deep cleansing breath wiped away my tears and took off. I started with a slow jog to warm up. I tried to clear my head of all thoughts but instead it filled up of images of him loving some other woman. She was getting everything from him that I ached for. My body was on auto pilot and my mind was in a trans. The more I ran the more I thought about him sexing her the faster I ran. I was like a rat on a wheel. By the time I was done it was nine a.m. I was completely exhausted physically and mentally. This was perfect timing because I knew that by the time I walked back home Rodney would have left for work and I wouldn't have to pretend that everything was alright. My nana used to say to me when I was a little girl that prayer heals all and answers all so if your going to pray don't worry but if your gonna worry don't make since to pray because your going to block your blessings by worrying. It's all about having faith. You have to have it.

I was doing all the wrong things. I didn't have faith and although I continuously prayed I worried just as much if not more.

Eleven forty-five I arrived at the place I was to meet the detective. I went inside the cyber café ordered two lattes and sat at a private computer off to the side. He and the coffee arrived at the same time. We waited for the waiter to leave then he looked at me. He placed a large manila envelope on the table and put his hands on top of it. Are you sure you want to go thru with this? Yes… I need to see her face. Before he handed me my package he told me they were meeting this evening at the Marriott in the east village at seven. Here is an extra key to the room they will be in. they always get the same room. The key is my gift to you free of charge. A friend of mine who works there owed me. If you decide to go thru with this the back door to the hotel will be open. I paid him and thanked him for all his help. I didn't dare open the package in public for fear of my own reaction. I decided to put the package up for safe keeping. Who needs pictures when I can have a face to face meeting. He can't deny anything if I Catch them in the act.

Totally exhausted I set the alarm clock for four p.m. and fell fast asleep.

I jumped up at the sound of the alarm, showered dressed in all black. I pulled my black shiny shoulder length mane into a tight bun grabbed my black shades and headed out the door. When I arrived at the Marriott I parked in the back in between two dumpsters so he wouldn't notice my car. Before I got out I hesitated and thought… this could get ugly, I better take some protection. With that I put on my shades and headed for the back door. Just like the detective said, it was open. I slipped in quietly closing the door behind me. I took the key out of my pocket it read room six thirty as I took the stairs to the sixth floor I thought…ain't that a bitch, six thirty is our wedding date. How dare they always get the same room number. What's that about I wondered? When I reached the sixth floor I waited until the voices I heard trailed off. When it was quiet I opened the door and peeked out. The hallway was clear. I found the room easily and quickly entered so as not to be seen by anyone. I flicked on the light and gasped at what I saw. There were fresh long stem pink and white roses and a card that read… to my true love… forever yours Rodney. I felt the tears well up in my eyes. There was wine chilling in an ice bucket on the table with two wine glasses. The king sized heart shaped bed was adorned with red rose pedals. This was so romantic. All the time I spent with this man I never even knew he had a romantic bone in his body. He never did any of these things for me. How dare him. I went from feeling hurt and hopeless to complete rage. All these years wasted. I didn't know him at all he was a complete stranger. He shared his deepest feelings and secrets with her, all of which I got none. I felt cheated and deceived. I felt a panic attack coming on. I told myself… no not now… calm down and just breathe. When it passed I found myself a hiding place in the closet which showed a view of the entire room. From the closet floor I could see and hear everything. I decided to wait until they were in the act to bust them. I glanced at my watch it read six fifty. They should be arriving any minute. I settled into my spot and waited. At seven ten I heard my husband's voice outside the door he was saying "cover your eyes no peeking" when he opened the door he told her to stay put I'll be right back. He came in took off his coat and draped it over the chair then he lit ten candles and placed them all about the room then turned off the light. There was pure excitement on his face. This was a side of him that I had never seen. For a fleeting moment sadness pained me. Then he brought her in. he guided her from behind standing in back of her with his hands around her waist. When they got to the spot he thought was perfect he leaned over her shoulder and kissed her softly on the neck. You can look now he said in his sexiest voice. She pulled her hands away from her eyes and gasped at the beautiful surroundings. Without saying a word she turned to face him. She threw her arms around his neck and gave him such a passionate kiss. From what I could see of her she had cocoa brown skin shoulder length hair they stood almost the same height and her frame was medium-small. For the most part his body blocked my view of her. That passionate kiss turned into roaming hands. Their lips never left each other all the while clothing started to fall to the floor. They became one big grouping moaning mass. He clapped his hands and the erotica c.d. I brought for us to spice our thing up started playing. He told me he couldn't get into it. It was all I could do to keep from bursting from the closet. I told myself just a few more minutes. I looked threw to find them naked on the bed. Rodney was lying face down and she was licking and sucking on the back of his neck slowly advancing towards his behind. When she got to his ass he arched it up and she dove in. I couldn't believe what I was seeing. I had to turn away. After a few minutes I heard him moan loudly which he always did when he penetrated me. The time had come for me to emerge from hiding. I burst from the closet and turned on the lights. What I saw horrified me. At first I froze then I vomited. Rodney jumped up baby I can explain. The hell you can! Not this time you can't. The woman spoke for the first time and her voice was deeper than Rodney's. I couldn't believe my eyes, I tried to blink the situation away but it was true. This woman had large breast like mine, pretty flowing hair like mine, Silky smooth skin like mine and a dick bigger than Rodney's.

  When I thought about everything I just saw at no time did I see anyone using protection. No plastic no condoms nothing. I saw red because we never used protection either. He was my husband and I thought that that was all the protection I needed. How could I have been so wrong? The he/she said "I don't want any parts of this; I already have a death sentence." Both Rodney and I stared at her/him with our mouths open because that statement needed no explanation. This motherfucker had AIDS. Rodney's eyes watered over. As he turned to me I drew my gun on both of them. Baby wait we can… he never got to finish his sentence because I shot him. Then

I turned my gun on the girl/guy as he was running out the door and fired my weapon. The bullet landed in his ass. Someone in the hotel heard the gun fire and called the cops. I didn't even try to run I just sat there trying to process all that had just unfolded in front of my eyes. Had I not seen it with my own eyes I wouldn't have believed it.

I was arrested and the other two went to the hospital for treatment. Nobody was hurt too badly, I'm not that good of a shooter. Rodney got hit in the thigh. The story hit the papers and the cops received an anonymous envelope that explained everything in detail of the events that led up to me shooting those fools. I was released from jail on temporary insanity charges. I immediately went to the clinic to get an HIV test. Thank God it was negative. I started taking prophylactic drugs when I was processed and I will continue to take them for the next year along with frequent testing. I didn't have to do much time in jail but I definitely am and will be seeing a therapist for a long time to come.

Printed in Great Britain
by Amazon